George Washington Johnson

Jottings by the Way

A Collection of Rustic Rhyme

George Washington Johnson

Jottings by the Way
A Collection of Rustic Rhyme

ISBN/EAN: 9783337270827

Printed in Europe, USA, Canada, Australia, Japan

Cover: Foto ©Andreas Hilbeck / pixelio.de

More available books at **www.hansebooks.com**

BY THE WAY

A COLLECTION OF RUSTIC RHYME

—BY—

GEO. W. JOHNSON;

WITH A BRIEF AUTOBIOGRAPHY.

CONTAINING ALSO,

SELECTIONS FROM THE WRITINGS OF OTHER

MEMBERS OF THE FAMILY.

ST. GEORGE, UTAH.

PRINTED BY C. E. JOHNSON.

1882.

"Virtus semper viridis."

Preface.

THIS small book is intended for a family keepsake, and not for the general public. Its pages are made up of odd bits of poetry and prose written under a variety of circumstances, and claim only the degree of merit they contain.

Therefore, gentle reader, shower thy criticisms lightly on their henceforth unprotected heads!

Should a few errors creep in, kindly bear in mind that you get them all for the same price, viz: .00.

The book is not copyrighted, hence the right-to-copy is not curtailed.

As a passing remark, we would say that the writers of the within do not write poetry for their daily bread.

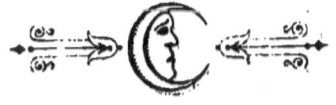

—TO—
ALL GOOD PEOPLE,
EVERYWHERE,
REGARDLESS OF CREED, SEX OR
NATIONALITY,
THIS VOLUME IS RESPECTFULLY
DEDICATED.

Index.

INDEX.

*** *Roman Numerals refer to Appendix.*

ERRATA.

Page 1, Last line of 1st verse, should read, "*In eighteen-thirty-one.*"

My mind has been wandering backward,
 Far back to the land of my birth
When tidings first reached us that angels
 Again had come back to the earth;—
And brought the glad news, that Jehovah
 His Latter-day work had begun,
And brought back the Priesthood to Joseph—
 In eighteen-sixty-one.

With joy we received the glad tidings
 That God by his servants had sent,
And gave them a home and a welcome,
 While they preached to the people—*Repent!*
And, as we believed in the message,
 We down to the water did go,
To follow the steps of the Saviour,—
 In eighteen-thirty-two.

We next up at Kirtland did gather;
 The Saints then in numbers were few,
But Joseph the Prophet was with us,
 And our hearts were all loyal and true.
He taught us that if we were faithful,
 Triumphant we always should be,
Our enemies never would conquer—
 (In eighteen-thirty-three.)

The Elders were sent to the nations,
 To spread the glad tidings abroad;

And the Saints were beginning to gather,
  To build up the Kingdom of God:
It was then we were told by the Prophet,
  That God would require, of our store
Our Tithing, to build up His Kingdom;
  (In eighteen-thirty-four.)

He taught us to love one another,
  And never be haughty or vain,
And leave off our pride and contentions,
  And from all bad habits refrain.
We there, to God's name built a Temple,
  And all for His blessings did strive—
And in it received our anointings,
  In eighteen-thirty-five.

We then were endowed with His spirit,
  The gifts to the Saints were restored,
And many received Revelations,
  While the tidings were scattered abroad.
The Saints were increasing in numbers,
  While Joseph, with others, did fix—
To strengthen the Stake in Missouri,
  In eighteen-thirty-six.

Our enemies gathered around us,
  And deserters arose in our band,
And the Prophet, with many more, left us
  For Missouri, our fair, Promised Land.
With the poor Saints we soon followed after,
  By mobs, from our homes we were driven,
But *we traveled*, through sickness and sorrow:—
  In eighteen-thirty-seven.

We next found ourselves left at Springfield
  To care for the sick and the dead;
But many continued their journey,
  Although without money or bread.
But God gave us friends in our trouble,

Who watched with us early and late,
Until we from sickness recovered,
In eighteen-thirty-eight.

Then the Saints from Missouri were driven,
From all their possessions, to roam;
And the leaders then crossed o'er the river,
At *Commerce* to find a new home.
Then again we were traveling westward,
To finish our former design
To dwell with the Saints and the Prophet,
In eighteen-thirty-nine.

At Commerce the Saints then did gather,
To build up the city—*Nauvoo;*
On the banks of the great Mississippi
A beautiful city soon grew;
For the Saints who were scattered did rally—
And to build up new homes soon begun;
For awhile they grew rich and did prosper—
In eighteen-forty-one.

We next built a town, called it *Ramus*—
(*a branch*)—twenty miles from Nauvoo,
Where we often did meet with the Prophet,
Who taught us some things that were new.
It was there that we learned the great secret
(That then was revealed to but few:)
Many wives we should marry if faithful,—
In eighteen-forty-two.

But dissenters soon sprung up among us,
Like Judas—our Prophet betrayed—
Amongst them ware those he had trusted,
And placed in high places to lead.
They scattered the seeds of dissension,
But soon from our midst they did flee,
To stir up the ire of the gentiles
In eighteen-forty-three.

We again built a Temple at Nauvoo;
 By toil it was finished at last,
But traitors and mobs gathered round us
 And the Prophet in prison was cast.
Then Joseph and Hyrum were murdered—
 (Their blood stains the Carthage Jail floor)
And stands as a witness against them
 In eighteen-forty-four.

Then our enemies poured in the city
 To pillage and plunder and rob;
And many crossed over the River,
 And left everything to the mob.
Then Brigham was chosen our leader;
 As the mob were determined to drive,
With a few he crossed over the River
 In eighteen-forty-five.

And many were left unprotected,
 By the mob they were sorely oppressed,
But they kept crossing over the River
 To find a new home in the west.
At Kanesville and old Winter Quarters,
 They stopped and for winter did fix--
In the spring to continue their journey
 In eighteen-forty-six.

The saints that remained in the city,
 were leaving as fast as they could,
To follow their friends to the mountains
 Where they could get clothing and food.
They scattered abroad through the country,
 In winter by mobs they were driven,
To find a new home in the mountains,
 In eighteen-forty-seven.

Then traitors set fire to the Temple,
 And soon it was burned to the ground,
To come up in judgment against them

In that day when the trumpet shall sound.
The few that remained in the city,
    As the season was getting so late,
Concluded to winter at Nauvoo
    In eighteen-forty-eight.

There was nothing but sad desolation,
    To meet with in passing around,
The beautiful city in ruins,
    The Temple burned down to the ground.
The Prophet and Patriarch murdered;
    Destruction before and behind,
And the saints driven out on the desert
    'Twas thus in eighteen-forty nine.

In the spring we moved forward to Kanesville,
    But found them in sorrow and gloom;
The cholera swept through the country,
    And many went down to the tomb.
But we toiled on through sickness and sorrow,
    Till the time of departure had come,
To follow our friends to the mountains
    In eighteen-fifty-one.

Soon our long tedious journey was over,
    Our trials of travel were passed;
We had found a new home in the mountains,
    To dwell with our brethren at last.
Since then twenty-nine years we've labored,
    In building up Zions stronghold,
In the year eighteen hundred and eighty,
    The Church was just fifty years old!

But what are those brave valiant heroes
    Who have followed their leader so long,
And fought the good fight for the kingdom
    When the battle was raging so strong.
But few are remaining among us,
The most of them sleep by the way--
    They have fallen brave Martyrs of Jesus
To come forth in the great coming day.

LIKES AND DISLIKES.

O who can imagine what plague and what bother,
  To try to write verses to satisfy others;
So varied their fancy no two can agree
  What style or what subject good verses should be.

For instance the Matron wants matter of fact—
  Inclined to be pious, from scandal intact;
While the Miss in her teens. must have love and
    romance,
  And rambles by moonlight and meeting by chance.

The maiden of uncertain age,-let me see—
  Mix equal parts, gossip, and scandal and tea;
For the lady of fashion, praise her beautiful face,
  A love of a bonnet, rings, diamonds and lace.

The Soldier, of skirmishes, battles and slaughter;
  The Sailor, of daring deeds done on the water.
The Banker of gold, and Broker of stocks;
  The Sportsman fast horses, the Miner of rocks.

The Gamester how easy his fortune is made;
  The Merchant of profit in barter and trade;
The Rumseller mixing his customers grog,
  Of jolly good fellows as drunk as a hog.

The Toper, as homeward he staggers along—
  If 'tis vulgar enough he is singing your song;
While the Parson will say it is all very well
  If it tells about Heaven and warns you from Hell.

The Farmer, green meadows and bright yellow grain,
  The Lady, of flowers that bloom on the plain;
The Doctor his drugs, and the Student his books,
  For the Swell, you must talk of his exquisite looks.

Then how can we make up our verses to suit,
  All grades from the Gentleman down to the Brute.
So I'll give up the problem and have no more bother,
  But will just suit myself, have no care for another.

CONTENTMENT.

I've a humble cottage home, where the Summer
    flowers bloom,
And an orchard with an arbor 'neath its bow, old
    friend;
I've a garden for the hoe where I water plant and
    sow,
And a little farm above for the plow, old friend.

I've a parlor and a hall, if a friend should chance to
    call,
And a wife within the cottage to preside, old friend;
I have children living near, the old cottage home to
    cheer,
And I've friends who dwell around on every side, old
    friend.

I can sit within my door, when my daily toil is o'er,
And feel thankful for the blessings in my reach, old
    friend;
And I think tho' light of purse, that my fate might
    still be worse,
And I profit by the lesson it does teach, old friend.

I have cast away my pride, and put flattery aside,
And I try to gather wisdom from above, old friend;
Then if you like my style, just call and sit awhile,
And I'll tell you what I hate and what I love, old
    friend.

I love a woman's voice when she makes kind words
    her choice,
And the prattle of the children at their play, old
    friend;
But I hate a scold or shrew, who finds nothing else to
    do,
But to tattle and make mischief all the day, old
    friend.

I love an honest man who is doing all he can,
To promote the joy and happiness of earth old
    friend;
But I hate the selfish curse who would rob me of my
    purse,
And will leave the earth no better for his birth old
    friend.

I love a well tried friend upon whom I can depend,
Who will kindly bring my faults unto my view, old
    friend;
But a traitor I despise who with flattery and lies,
Will deceive each one with whom he has to do, old
    friend.

"AS MERRY AS A SCHOOL-GIRL."

As merry as a school girl I have often heard them
    say,
But I never knew its meaning until this very day,
I saw her going down the street, with satchel on her
    arm,
And oh, the merry song she sang, it did my senses
    charm.

It told me that her heart was light, it told me she
    was free,
From all the cares and ills of life that haunted those
    like me;
It minded me of by gone years, when I was but a
    child,
With heart as free and just as light and spirits just
    as wild.

When I like her was off to school with satchel on my
    arm,
With not a care to grieve the heart, but every thing
    to charm;

But oh those days are long since past and life is
    nearly o'er,
But oft I think of those bright days that will return
    no more.

A DOLLAR OR TWO.

Ye poets may sing of the power of dimes,
    And call their possession the greatest of crimes;
But tell me, without them what good could we do?
    I'm sure I'd be glad of a dollar or two.

In the shop you see something you really desire,
    A present for wife you have oft wished to buy her;
You feel in your pockets, what more can you do?—
    In hopes you may there find a dollar or two.

You go to the restaurant for a square meal,
    Your stomach is empty quite hungry you feel;
Your pockets are empty it makes you feel blue,
    How then would you fancy a dollar or two.

You are sick and discouraged and likely to die,
    You call in the doctor as he passes by;
You want his advice and his medicine too,
    But he is in want of a dollar or two.

Your lawyer will tell you your case is quite clear,
    He'll soon get you free, you have nothing to fear
When he pockets the fee he's expecting from you;
    But you languish in jail for a dollar or two.

Then may it be ever my fortune to hold,
    A few precious dollars in Silver or Gold;
For in this hard world it is pleasant to view,
    The bright, shining face of a dollar or two.

All men seek to win them—the root of all evil,
    It makes some a Heaven, sends some to the Devil;
Yet 'tis pleasant to hear, as we pass the world through,
    The ring and the chink of a dollar or two.

THE CHILDREN.

What is home, without the children
  Crowding 'round the cottage hearth,
With their eyes forever beaming,
  Full of laughter, joy and mirth?
Sunny hair, in ringlets, flowing
  O'er a neck of pearly white,
Little fingers, bent on mischief,
  Never still, from morn till night.

Home is lonely without children,
  How we miss their noisy mirth,
How we miss their gentle footsteps,
  Sitting, lonely, 'round our hearth,
How we miss their noisy prattle,
  And their joyous, childish glee,
How we miss their fond caresses,
  As they sit upon our knee.

When the evening shadows gather,
  And the daily toil is o'er;
How we miss their noisy greeting,
  At our humble cottage door.
Heaven bless the darling children,
  Though they are a constant care,
They will be the brightest jewels,
  In the crown we hope to wear.

SPRING.

Spring is coming, bees are humming
    In the fragrant air;
Birds are singing, bells are ringing,
    All is bright and fair.

Flowers are blooming, and perfuming,
    Nature all is bright;
Tendrils twining, bright sun shining,
    Shedding golden light.

Shady bowers, summer flowers,
　　Scattered o'er the plain,
Dew drops glisten, and we listen,
　　To the summer rain.

Singing birds, lowing herds,
　　Come with beauteous spring,
Opening flowers, summer showers,
　　Summer months will bring.

Yellow leaves, golden sheaves,
　　In the autumn day.
Winter cold, young and old,
　　Dance the time away.

A DREAM OF HOME.

I dreamed I was a boy again,
　　And on my mother's knee,
I listened to the fervent prayer,
　　She offered up for me.
Again I saw my childhood home—
　　The place that gave me birth,
And friends and kindred grouped around
　　The old, familiar hearth.
The Bible lay upon the stand,
　　Just as it used to do,
When I was in my childhood home,
　　Just fifty years ago.

The old dutch clock hung on the wall,
　　The cupboard too, was there,
The pictures on the mantelpiece,
　　And Mother's old arm chair.
Again I wandered through the wood,
　　Where oft in childhood's hours
I sauntered forth to gather nuts, .
　　Or cull the fragrant flowers.
I rambled o'er the meadow, too,
　　Where berries used to grow,

'Twas just the same as when a boy,
    Just fifty years ago.

The orchard, too, where oft I've sat,
    And watched the busy bee,
Was just the same—the bees were there,
    As they were wont to be.
The barn, the cornhouse, and the spring
    Where oft, in summer's day,
I've knelt beside to get a drink,
    When tired of boyish play;
The Gulf-lot, where I drove the cows,
    As I to school did go,
To learn to read, and write, and spell,
    Just fifty years ago.

Ah me! that was a happy dream,
    My dream of childhood's hours,
When all the thorns of life had gone,
    And left the brightest flowers.
But those bright days will no more come,
    While I on earth remain;
My childhood's home, my early friends,
    I ne'er shall see again.
A few more days of toil and strife,
    And I'll be called, to go
To join the friends I loved so well,
    Just fifty years ago!

A ROSE, IN OCTOBER.

Sweet Rose! in thy fragrance and beauty I found thee,
When all thy dear kindred had faded away,
When cold, dreary winter was hovering 'round thee,
And frost on thy petals like diamonds did play!

Sweet flower! I'll not leave thee to pine in thy beauty,
To wither and die by the frost, in a day,
I'll take thee where kind, gentle eyes will behold thee,
Thy beauty admire, till thy leaves drop away!

LIFE'S SHADOWS.

There are times in our lives, when, with sadness and
gloom,
Our minds are o'ershadowed, and dark as the tomb;
When joy, hope and gladness, have faded away,
And left us, in darkness, to grope on our way;
But let's not despair, or at fortune be whining,
For every dark cloud has a bright, silver lining.

Tho' fortune is fickle, and friends are untrue,
And fate seems against you, and pleasures seem few,
Tho' dark are the clouds, that o'ershadow thy way,
Press on! do not heed what the tempter may say;
Don't falter nor stumble, or e'er be repining,
For the darker the cloud is, the brighter the lining!

Though your friends may seem few, and your fortune
adverse,
Look around! you'll see many whose fate is much worse;
'Tis to teach us this lesson that trials we meet:
If we taste not the bitter, we know not the sweet!
Be patient, the sun will soon brightly be shining,
And show you the cloud had a *bright, silver lining!*

AN "OLD FOGY" MORMON.

They may call me "Old Fogy," whenever they will,
Or "Stereotyped Mormon," for good or for ill;
Such names, to another, might give great offence,
But to me, it shows talking of *good, common sense.*

I'm proud to inform them, for many long years,
I have waded through sorrow, affliction and tears;
And have stood by the side of the Prophet of God,
When traitorous enemies sought his heart's blood.

And many a time did I list to his voice,
When the words he did utter, caused me to rejoice;
He taught to us lessons of light, and of truth,
I have treasured them up since the days of my youth.

He told us of hard times quite near at our door,
  Of blessings which God for His Saints had in store;
Of sorrows and happiness, joys, and of tears,
Not one Prophecy failed, *I have watched fifty years!*

And I ever will cherish his memory, dear,
  Till I finish the mission he left for me here;
Then call me "old fogy," I'll make no complaint,
While it means, an old Veteran Latter-Day Saint.

TIME IS FLEETING.

Time is precious, use it wisely,
  Idle not the hours away;
Years are made of little moments,
  Grasp, and use them while you may.

Time is fleeting; every moment
  Let some noble deed be done;
When 'tis passed 'tis gone forever,
  Years are passing, one by one.

Every moment there is something,
  That your hands may find to do,
That will lighten some-one's burden,
  And a blessing bring to you.

There are always those around you,
  Who may need your help or care,
Sinking hearts are always near you,
  And the poor are everywhere;

Feed the hungry, clothe the needy,
  Pleasure to the poor impart,
Gentle words, that cost you nothing,
  Oft-times raise the sinking heart.

Never falter in well doing,
  Labor with your hands and brain;
Kind words, spoken to the erring,
  Sometimes bring them back again.

When the years of life are numbered,
  And your sun is nearly set;
Leave no stains in life behind you,
  That may cause you sad regret.

Let your life be spent, in doing
  Good to all, and harm to none,
So you calmly may resign it,
  Knowing all has been well done.

THE INDIAN TO HIS STEED.

Brave steed! thy work at last is done;
  No more thy nimble feet
Will wander o'er the pastures green,
  So graceful, and so fleet.
Thou'st borne me many a weary mile,
  Upon thy sturdy back,
And oft have been my hope and stay,
  Upon the desert track.

Thou hast been ever brave and true—
  Thy courage did not flee;
And when my life endangered was,
  You was *most true* to me.
When danger lurked along my path
  Thy fleetness bore me through;
Well could I trust thee, faithful steed,
  For thou wert tried and true.

Thou'st served me well for many years,
  Through many dangers passed;
But age came on, and cruel *Death*
  Has cut thee down at last!
No more I'll mount thee, faithful steed,
  No more I'll danger dare;
For I, like thee am growing old—
  Thy fate I soon must share.

REMEMBER THE POOR.

Cold Winter is coming, there's frost in the air,
  The beautiful Summer has passed;
The flowers are all dying, that once were so fair,
  Their fragrance has gone with the blast.
The tops of the mountains are covered with snow,
  The North wind comes under your door,
Then, (if you are able to pay what you owe,)
  Be sure to Remember the Poor!

Cold Winter is coming, his footsteps are near;
  He will spread desolation around,
And make the Earth dreary, and frosty, and sere,
  And scatter the snow o'er the ground.
The leaves have turned yellow, and fall'n from the
    trees,
  The bountiful harvest is o'er;
The beautiful brooks are beginning to freeze,
  'Tis time to Remember the Poor!

Cold Winter is coming—where plenty abounds
  The dance and the song will be heard;
With mirth and with music your halls will resound,
  And many will bow at your word;
Then, remember the poor, let their hearts be made
    glad,
  By something you spare from your store;
It will nourish the feeble, and cheer up the sad,—
  Be sure to Remember to the Poor!

Cold Winter is coming, his cold, icy breath,
  Is whistling through mountain and dell;
All nature he'll touch with the finger of Death,
  And lock up the earth with his spell.
He will laugh at the needy, and mock at the poor,
  As widely he opens their door;
So try to spare something,—a mite every day
  A blessing will seem, to the Poor.

TO A BEREAVED MOTHER.*

Six little graves lay side by side, all from one moth-
    er's fold,
In one short month they all had died, were laid be-
    neath the mold;
How much of grief a heart may bear, this mother well
    may know,
By death's cold icy hand to lay them in the grave so
    low.

There is a hope for those that weep for friends who've
    gone before,
To meet them in a brighter land, where parting is no
    more,
Where death and sorrow never come to mar our hap-
    piness,
Where love and peace and joy abound, in one eternal
    bliss.

Then may this hope inspire your heart, to help you
    bear the pain,
To feel the loss to you so great, to them is clearly gain,
That when your earthly work is done and all your
    troubles o'er,
You then will meet your babes again, where parting
    is no more.

*Six children from one family died of Diphtheria
within two weeks.

WILL THEY MISS ME.

Will they miss me at home will they miss me,
    When I am laid low on my bier?
Will they silently gather around me
    And drop on my coffin a tear?

Will they miss me around the home fireside,
    When the shadows of night o'er them creep:

When the children retire to their slumbers,
  Will they miss me to watch o'er their sleep?

When the children return to the Homestead
  Will they miss me around the lone hearth;
When they think of the one that is absent,
  Will a shadow come over their mirth?

Will they think of the words I have spoken,
  And say he was always our friend;
And although he was plain and outspoken,
  He loved us, each one, to the end?

Will they kindly look over my actions
  And say, though his faults were not few,
He never intended to wrong us,
  His heart was still loving and true?

Will they use all my faults as a beacon
  To steadily guide their own barque,
And shun all the rocks I have wrecked on,
  Though the way may be stormy and dark?

'Tis enough, if they know all my actions
  Were prompted for ultimate good;
And if I have failed in my purpose,
  I have done for them all that I could.

BOYHOODS FRIENDS.

Our boyhoods friends are dying; yes, one by one they go,
The most of them are lying beneath the sod so low;
They're resting from their labors, the friends we loved
      so well,
Along the road we've traveled, their mouldering bodies
      dwell.

We sigh to see them leaving and sinking in the grave,
We've known them from our childhood, their hearts
      were true and brave;
The good old friends we've cherished from boyhood's
      early day,

How can we help but shed a tear to see them pass
   away.

A few of them still wander along life's dreary way,
But one by one they're leaving and passing fast away;
And soon Death's icy hand will touch each heart so
   brave,
And lay each friend of boyhood into a silent grave.

And thus doth time draw wrinkles where youth's bright
   smiles hath played,
Our star of hope scarce twinkles ere it begins to fade;
We too, are growing old, our locks are mixed with
   gray,
Ere many winters more, we too will pass away.

Then let us up and doing and battle in the strife,
And finish up our mission, and do our part in life,
That when our work is ended, we'll know it is well
   done,   [ready gone.
That we may rest in peace with friends, who have al-

FIVE FACES ON THE WALL.

THOUGHTS ON SEEING A GROUP OF PORTRAITS OF THE BROTHERS
JOEL H., JOS. E., BENJ. F., GEO. W. AND WILLIAM D. JOHNSON.

I see on the ceiling five faces together,
They are all that is left of the sons of our mother;
And as time flies away, but a few years at best,
Ere they all in the grave for a season must rest.

In the kingdom of God they have toiled many years,
And shared in its blessings, its sorrows and tears;
With Joseph the Prophet, they have battled for truth,
And strove for the right since the days of their youth.

They have stood by his side when the battle was strong,
And have fought for the truth 'gainst oppression and
   wrong,
Till they saw him laid low in the cold silent grave,
And they knew that his heart was true, valiant and
   brave.

And they knew that the hands that were stained with
    his blood,
Had willfully martyred a prophet of God;
And they knew, like a lamb to the slaughter, he went,
For warning all men of their sins to repent.

And through life they have followed the precepts he
    taught,
Until age has come on and life's battles are fought;
Still they know that his words have been true and
    sincere,
And they always will cherish his memory dear.

In the years that remain may they feel no regret,
But be firm in the cause until life's sun is set;
When their mission is filled, may they meet him again,
In a far better land beyond sorrow and pain.

THE OLD KIRTLAND TEMPLE.

Thou grand old pile! thy fame is spread
    From land to land and sea to sea,
Where'er the gospel light is shed,
    The Saints have read or heard of thee.

How oft in childhood's happy hours,
    Ere thy foundation stone was laid,
Where thou art reared with dome and tower,
    Upon that very spot I've played.

Jehovah spake! the work began,
    And soon thy tower on high was reared;
There God again communed with man,
    There we have oft His name revered.

How oft within thy walls we've heard
    The meek and lowly Prophet's voice,
And as we listened to his words,
    O how it made our hearts rejoice.

How oft beneath thy roof we've met
  To serve the Lord in praise and prayer,
And as we worshipped at His feet,
  How oft we've felt His presence there.

But strangers pass thy portals now,—
  But oft my thoughts will wander there
To where the Prophet oft did bow
  Beneath thy roof in humble prayer.

TO ADA.*

We have laid her away in the cold silent tomb,
And our hearts are o'ershadowed with sadness and
    gloom;
We have turned from the place with a sad heavy heart,
For 'tis hard with our dear little treasures to part.

But we know that the angels have taken her home,
Where sickness and sorrow can never more come;
She is free from temptation, she now is at rest,
And God in His wisdom has done for the best.

How sadly we'll miss her around the lone hearth,
Her smile and her laughter, her prattle and mirth;
Her raiment, her toys, her companions and all,
Will often remind us and tear drops will fall.

And then at the table how lonely 'twill be,
There her sweet little face we shall never more see;
The bed where she slumbered, the pillow she pressed,
And the prayers that she murmered retiring to rest.

But God in His wisdom has called her away,
Then why should we murmer or wish her to stay
In this cold dreary-world filled with sorrow and pain,
When we know that ere long we shall meet her again?

Died April 13, 1882.

OLD FRIENDS.

One by one they are leaving, are passing away,
The friends I have cherished in life's early day;
Side by side through this life we have toiled on for
    years,
And shared with each other its joys and its tears,
Until time in its flight hath dropped snow on our hair,
And left on our faces the traces of care;
But a few more short years and this life will be o'er,
And we'll all meet again on a far brighter shore.

THE GOOD OLD YANKEE DOODLE.

Yankee Doodle is the tune some Yankee chap invented,
To sing on Independence Day to make us feel con-
    tented;
Now Independence day has come, as many have be-
    fore us,
We'll sing again the good old tune and all join in the
    chorus.
    Yankee Doodle is the tune the Mormons find so
      handy
    To sing on Independence Day, old Yankee Doodle
      Dandy.
The Mormons are a jolly set, they come from every
    nation,
From every country, every clime, in all this broad
    creation;
They all believe in serving God just as they have a
    mind to,
And marry one wife, two, or three, just as they feel
    inclined to.
They all believe that Washington the founder of the
    nation,
Was called of God to do that work and led by in-
    spiration;
They think the laws our Fathers made, were what they
    were intended;

They've stood the test a hundred years and need not
    be amended.

There are some fellows now so smart they've got it in
    their noodle,
That Mormon Boys can take the lead in playing Yan-
    kee Doodle;
So they are trying very hard to make a clear solution,
By tearing up old Seventy-six and change the Con-
    stitution.

Then let us our own business mind, that is the Mor-
    mon Creed sir,
And when the race is run, they'll find the Mormons in
    the lead, sir;
Then let them tell what lies they will, we'll show the
    whole caboodle,
That we are Loyal Citizens, to the tune of Yankee
    Doodle.

THE CHAIRS THAT ARE VACANT TO-NIGHT.

It is Christmas again at the old cottage Home,
    There is bustle around the old hearth,
The children again are beginning to come
    To join in its pleasure and mirth;
The table is loaded with food of the best,
    And each one seems filled with delight,
But a shadow comes over each one as we think
    Of the chairs that are vacant to-night.

In the years that are passed when the hollidays come,
    The children have always been here
To join in the sports at the old cottage home,
    And partake of its mirth and good cheer;
But they now are not here, some have wandered away,
    We miss them our circle to light;
Their absence has caused a deep shadow to-day,
    For their chairs will be vacant to-night.

But we hope when another bright Christmas shall come
  We shall all be together once more,
Beneath the dear roof of the old cottage home,
  Where so oft we have gathered before,
To enjoy all the pleasures the holidays give,
  That our hearts may be happy and light;
May no shadow come over our hearts as we think
  That no chairs will be vacant to-night.

SUPPLICATION.

Oh thou mighty God of Jacob
  Listen to my humble prayer,
As I bow the knee before Thee,
  Wilt thou take me in thy care.

Wilt thou grant me my petition?
  I will ask Thee not for wealth,
But oh, give me, Heavenly Father,
  The rich blessings, Life and Health.

I ask not for worldly honor,
  I ask not for worldly fame,
But instead, oh! Father give me
  With thy Servants, a good name.

I will ask Thee not for power,
  I will ask Thee not for might,
But instead, oh give me wisdom,
  To direct me in the right.

Help me in my daily labor
  To provide for every need,
And inspire my heart to serve thee,
  And thy laws and counsels heed.

When my mission here is ended,
  And my earthly labor o'er,
Bring me back into thy presence,
  There to dwell forevermore.

This I ask through Christ our Saviour,
Who our sins and sorrows bore,
And I'll give to Thee the honor
And the glory evermore.

OUR MOUNTAIN HOME.

Deseret! Deseret! 'tis our own Mountain Home,
Where the Saints from all countries and nations have
come;
Where the fish to be caught, in the parable net,
Are all gathering here in our fair Deseret.

We are here from all countries, all nations and climes,
For we plainly can see by the signs of the times,
That the fig tree has blossomed, the summer has set;
We are waiting His coming, in fair Deseret.

From Settlement, County and State we've been driven;
We have asked for redress but no favor was given;—
To plan our destruction in council they met,
Ere we came to the valley of fair Deseret.

But our foes have resolved (with an eye to the spoil,)
To possess all we've gained by our labor and toil;
And our Rulers, with falsehood and lies have beset,
To disfranchise the Saints in our fair Deseret.

But our God at the helm will direct us aright;
We will trust to His arm through the dark stormy
night;
We have faith in his promise, we will trust to him yet,
He will steer us safe through, in our fair Deseret.

FREEDOM AND LIBERTY.

Thank God there are true, noble men in the land,
By the old Constitution who firmly will stand;
Brave chieftains of battle for freedom and right,
In the strife 'gainst oppression, who nobly will fight.

Fight on, valiant heroes! thy names shall be spread
On our history's page with the heroes that bled,
And fought for our liberty, freedom and right
When the dear Constitution was framed in its might.

Thy cause is a just one, the poor and oppressed
Will remember the names of Brown, Morgan, and Vest,
In the halls of our Congress, who fears not to face
The oppressor who dares the old flag to disgrace!

Then hurrah for the Banner! unfurl it on high!
Let it float on the breeze while we send up the cry
For Freedom and Liberty over the land,
While the old Constitution unsullied shall stand.

THE LITTLE ONES.

The little ones are coming
    I hear their noisy feet,
I hear their childish prattle
    As they come down the street.
They are coming down to grandpa's
    For an hour or two to-day,
To ramble in the orchard,
    And around the old house play.

They will pull the things to pieces,
    And will scatter them about;
They will make the old time music,
    The children's laugh and shout:
They will be in every mischief,
    Their little hands can find,
They know I'll scold a little,
    But that they do not mind.

Their father and their mother,—
    How short the time to me,
Since they were little children.
    And sitting on my knee;

They grew to men and women
　And found themselves new homes,
And now to cheer the old one,
　Their little children come.

God bless the little children,
　Long may they live to come,
To cheer the lonely cottage
　That was their parents' home;
While I remain, their presence
　Will ever welcome be,
And when I'm gone they'll miss me,
　And shed a tear for me.

THIS GOOD OLD WORLD.

The world is not so bad a world
　As many people take it;
'Tis just as good, and just as bad,
　As we poor mortals make it.
If all the people in the world
　Would do unto each other
As each would like to have them do,
　And treat each like a brother,

The world would then be filled with joy,
　And sorrow would be banished,
And hatred would be turned to love,
　And all our troubles vanished.
The time that now is spent in crime,
　Would then be spent in labor,
And each one then would be as rich
　And happy as his neighbor.

The time that's spent in hunting crime,
　The time that's spent to do it,
The time that's spent to punish crime
　And all that's wasted through it,

If it was spent in honest toil
  And doing good to others,
We'd all be rich and all be wise,
  And live like honest brothers.

One half the world now follow crime
  For wealth, or pride, or passion;
The other half, with honest toil,
  Support them in that fashion;
It will be thus until the day
  Of final separation;
The wicked then will be destroyed,
  The righteous rule the nation.

RETROSPECTIVE. JUNE 13, 1881.

Just thirty years ago to-day, I left my Eastern home,
With wives and children and with friends, o'er desert
    lands to roam;
'Twas then I left my mother dear, her face to see no
    more,
My brothers, sisters, and my friends, so dear in days
    of yore.

I bid adieu to all that day, and started for the West,
To seek a home far o'er the plains, where whiteman's
    foot ne'er pressed,
Where free from turmoil and from strife, from mobs
    and tyrants' reign,
I left my home and friends so dear, and started o'er
    the plain.

Three months upon the plains we toiled, to reach the
    mountain dell,
And oh! the hardships we endured, no human tongue
    can tell;
These thirty years how changed the scenes, the young
    have all grown old,
The old who have not passed away, their years will
    soon be told.

The desert where the wild beast trod, now blossoms
    like the rose,
And where the red man roamed the plain, we dwell in
    sweet repose:
The waving grain, the tree, the vine, that now adorns
    the land,
All show to us we have been led by God's protecting
    hand.

DOLLARS AND DIMES.

I've been thinking to-day of what absolute sway,
    In these hard and unreasonable times,
Of so simple a thing as the clear pleasant ring
    Of the powerful Dollars and Dimes.

No power so strong can compete with its song,
    Against the bright ring and the chimes;
It holds a full sway and will carry the day,—
    The ring of the Dollars and Dimes.

If an office you crave, you can scarcely it have;
    Although hard for the poor are the times;
If your purse is replete, you can never be beat,
    If you "shell out" the Dollars and Dimes.

At the bar you appear, your guilt is quite clear,
    There are plenty will list to the chimes,
That their memories will brighten, till they can en-
    lighten
    The jury, for Dollars and Dimes.

Though arrested and tried, ere the case they decide,
    You need have no fears of the times;
You will surely get clear, if your best friends are near,—
    The powerful Dollars and Dimes.

Though in prison you lie and are likely to die,
    No matter how great are your crimes;

Though your fate may be sealed, it may yet be appealed,
   If you've plenty of Dollars and Dimes.

But the want of the ring of this powerful thing,
   Has sent good men to prison sometimes;
And there they may lie, to languish and die,
   For the want of the Dollars and Dimes.

May the day come again when the powerful reign
   Of the ring, and the chink, and the chimes,
May be shorn of their might and be used for the right—
   These powerful Dollars and Dimes.

THE TWELFTH OF JANUARY.

I am thinking to-day of the years that have passed,
That has brought this day round every year, to the last;
And I kindly remember each one of our race,
And the many events to this day we can trace.

'Twas this day our Father was born,—records say,
And married our Mother on this very day;
They also inform us a Sister was born,
And our dear Father died on this day, in the morn.

One grand-child was married on this noted day,
And what more has happened I'm sure I can't say;
In the years that have passed we have oft met together,
And a good, social time we have had with each other.

But relations and friends are all passing away,
And but few now remain who remember the day;
And while I shall live, as this day passes o'er,
I will cherish kind thoughts of those dear friends of
   yore.

JOSEPH SMITH, THE PROPHET.

He was a man of sterling worth,
   And true to friend or brother,
And always taught us to be true

And kind to one another.
He told us pride, and haughtiness,
    And vanity were evil,
And all who would indulge in them
    Were prompted by the Devil.
He told us fashion led astray,
    And Saints would never love it,
That God had made us in His form,
    And man could not improve it.
He taught us to refrain from sin,
    And practice good behavior,
And imitate the pattern of
    Our meek and lowly Saviour.

ODE TO MY OLD COAT.

Thou dear old coat, with which I've passed
Through many a storm and wint'ry blast,
        I'll hang behind the door!
Cold winter's past, and summer's near,
From cold I now have naught to fear,
        From snow, or tempest's power.
Thou'st served me long, and served me well,
Thy worth, old coat, I cannot tell;
        Thou wert my only friend.
With thee I've trod the Road of Life,
Wrapped snug in thee when storms were rife,
        Thou did'st much comfort lend;
Thou art now much the worse for wear,
Art patched and mended here and there --
        With cloth of varied hue;
But these mischances fell on thee
In the good cause of serving me—
        Since thou wer't bright and new;
Old friend, think not these marks of wear
Will cause me for thee less to care;
        Thou art no Summer friend!

But thou art dearer, far, to me,
Than gaudy silk could ever be,
      On thee I could depend!
How different thou from men; the while
The Sun of Fortune shines, they smile,
      But let a cloud appear,
They're off like chaff—thou art a warm,
Kind-hearted friend in every storm;
      With thee, I need not fear.
Farewell old friend, but think thou not
That thou wilt ever be forgot
      Through Summer's sultry reign.
Like me thou'rt getting old and worn,
On many a snag we have been torn,
      I'll use thee oft again.

MY MOTHER'S LOVE.

O how my heart yearns for a mother's caresses,
  As when in childhood by sickness laid low,
When she swept my wan face with her dark silver
    tresses,
  And printed a kiss on my feverish brow.

How firm and untiring she watched by my pillow,
  'Till the long weary night with its shadows had flown,
And the day god arose over mountain and billow,
  And relieved her night vigils so patiently borne.

How kind were her accents, how gentle her chiding,
  How sweet was her smile and how fervent her prayer;
Her love was unselfish, so pure and abiding,
  How patient her toiling, how watchful her care.

The love of a mother abideth forever,
  It clings to the heart when all others have flown;
In all of earths trials *forget it*, no never!
  No love like a mother's love ever was known!

THE LOAFER.

Who saunters out upon the street,
To laugh, and chat, with those he meets,
And light and smoke his cigarette?
    The Loafer.

And when he finds a pleasant shade,
That some good neighbor's trees have made,
Who sits and plies his pocket blade?
    The Loafer.

Who sits, and smokes, and whittles on,
Until his cigarette is gone,
And then who makes *another one?*
    The Loafer.

And when the sun is getting hot,
Who'll rise and saunter from the spot
To some one's house, (his own 'tis not)?
    The Loafer.

Who, seated in the easy chair,
Will make so free you would declare
That he must be the Gov'nor there?
    The Loafer.

Whose patient wife at home must stay,
To toil and labor all the day,
While he is idling time away?
    The Loafer's.

MY FIFTY-NINTH BIRTHDAY.

And can it be, so many years have really passed away,
That I am fifty-nine years old on this my natal day,
That age is really coming on and life is nearly o'er,
And all my boyhood years are gone, to come to me no
  more?

I feel the same impulses still, of sorrow and of joy,
Of hope, of happiness and love, as when I was a boy;

But then the labor and the toil, my limbs will not perform,
My sight is dim, my hearing dull, my brow with fur-
rows worn,
My body bent, my dark brown hair is silvered o'er
with gray,
All tell me I am growing old, all tokens of decay;
Then when from earth I'm called to go, may friends
be gathered near,
To lay me calmly in the grave and drop the parting
tear.

THE HOME I'D LOVE.

(*To my Boys.*)

Go boys and find a better land, a home for you and me,
Where we can go and dwell in peace, from noise and
bustle free,
Where you can raise your little ones in wisdom's
pleasant ways,
And I in peace and quietude may finish out my days.

You know I'm growing old, my boys, and soon shall
pass away;
Then let me live a peaceful life, the few years I may
stay;
And when my earthly work is done and all my trials
o'er,
I'll leave a father's blessing, boys, if I can do no more.

I want a little fertile land, the acres may be few,
Enough to raise my daily bread,—that I must surely do,
For I would labor for my bread while life and health
remain,
I would not live by charity while toil my wants will
gain.

I want my children living near, their faces I must see,
For life would give but little joy, if they were far from
me;

For when I'm called from earth away to take my final
    rest,
I know they'd lay me gently down with flowers upon
    my breast.
I've always wished for such a home and hoped it would
    be mine
When I had passed my manhood years and come to
    life's decline,
And should it chance to be my lot, 'twould smooth
    the path of life,
And give me strength to labor on, and lessen toil and
    strife.

FASHION. THE LADY OF THE PERIOD.

Oh, what a state the world is in, and still is getting
    worse;
With pride and fashion bearing rule, society's great
    curse;
You meet a lady on the street, O don't she put on airs,
It took eighteen or twenty yards to make the dress
    she wears.

'Tis trimmed with ruffles, tucks and frills, with rib-
    bons and with lace;
And over all she wears a coat that any swell would
    grace;
The jaunty hat upon her head with flowers is laden
    down,
And underneath she wears a braid that fills a magic
    crown.

And O the jewels that she wears of gold would break
    a bank;
You gaze upon her and you think: "a lady sure, of
    rank;"
But list awhile and hear her talk, you soon will change
    your mind;

She to the lower class belongs, you by her talk will
    find.

She meets a lady on the street -"Good morning Mrs.
    S.,
It seems an age since last we met, Oh what a splendid
    dress!
'Tis green—the very shade I love; and what a splen-
    did fit!
Pray tell me where you found the goods, I must have
    one like it!"

She passes on; the next she meets is "dearest Mrs. J.,
O dear, I'm glad we meet again, pray how are you
    to-day?
Oh what a lovely dress, my dear, did you meet Mrs.
    S ?
I met her, just a moment since, in such a *horrid* dress!

In such a suit, upon the street *I* never would be seen,
The style and fashion ages old, and, would you think
    it—*green !"*
And thus she flatters every one, with vanity and lies,
When out of sight, the next she meets, the last she'll
    criticise.

But when at home the scene has changed--extrava-
    gance and dress,
With pride and fashion, have consumed domestic hap-
    piness.
Now if such women still must move in good society,
Good, honest wives will soon become a thing that
    used to be.

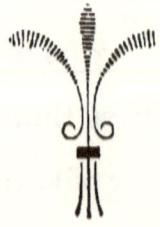

APPENDIX.

A BRIEF AUTOBIOGRAPHY OF
GEORGE WASHINGTON JOHNSON.

I was born at Pomfret, Chatauqua Co., New York, on the Nineteenth of February, 1823; my father's name was Ezekiel Johnson, my mother's, Julia Hills. Of their ancestors I know but little. They were born and married in the State of Massachusetts, and in the year 1812, with seven children, moved to the western part of New York, (then a new country,) where they settled, and reared a family of 16 children: nine sons and seven daughters. My Mother was a devout Presbyterian, and raised her family in strict observance of the precepts of the Bible. She was loved and respected by all who knew her. She died at Council Bluffs Iowa, a firm believer in the religious doctrines taught by the Prophet Joseph Smith.

During the winter of 1831, my brother Joel came from Ohio, bringing with him the *Book of Mormon.* Other Elders soon followed, and the result was, that my Mother and some of her children were baptized. About this time, Elder James Brackenbury, then on a mission, was taken sick and died at our house. He was buried at Laona. Fearing that the body might be disturbed, two of my brothers determined to watch the grave; during the night an attempt was made to steal the remains, which, (being nearly accomplished) their timely arrival prevented. The miscreants fled— were pursued, and one captured but never brought to justice.

In the Spring of 1833 we moved to Kirtland, Ohio, where the Latter-day Saints were then gathering. It was here that I, with the other younger members of our family, was baptised; here we became acquainted with the Prophet, Joseph Smith, and other authorities of the Church; here we witnessed the "falling of the stars," a magnificent meteoric shower, in 1833, also the building and dedication of the Kirtland Temple; here I received my Patriarchal Blessing, under the hands of Joseph Smith, Sen.; here we buried four members of our family, one of whom (Seth) accompanied the Prophet to Missouri in what was known as "Zion's Camp;"—their names were: Nancy, Seth, David, and Susan; here we passed through all the persecution that resulted in the expulsion of the Saints.

In the Spring of 1838 we started for Missouri in what was known as "Kirtland Camp," consisting of all the poor then remaining at Kirtland, and all who were able and willing to help them. The company embraced about 800 souls, all in straitened circumstances, with sixty wagons. The trip was a very trying one, as we were often destitute of food, and there was much sickness among us. At Dayton, Ohio, we stopped a few weeks to work on the National Turnpike, to obtain food and allow the sick to recuperate.

Threats were made that we "should not pass through Mansfield, (a small town on our route) alive." We started along, however, in close procession; the women driving the teams, and the men walking alongside; on nearing the town we were met by two horsemen who rode down each side of our column, seeming to count the wagons and soon returned to the town. Ere this, our ears had detected the beating of drums and firing of cannon, but we pushed on, and were not molested. We afterwards learned that the horsemen had given to the crowd who had assembled in front of the Court House, and were there firing the cannon, a very exaggerated report of our numbers and armament.

On reaching Springfield, Illinois, Samuel Hale died, leaving, in our care, a wife and daughter. It was decided to leave the sick here for the present, and my brothers Joel and Joseph were selected to remain and care for them, while my brother Benjamin continued to assist in the care of the company on their journey to Far West.

During the winter following we had a great amount of sickness; sister Hale died, and my Mother adopted her only daughter, (Mary Ann.)

In the Spring of 1839 we again started westward to gather with the Saints at Nauvoo, Illinois, but when we arrived within twenty miles thereof, it was thought best to remain and build a town at a place previously known as Perkins' Settlement, but which was then changed to Ramus, and, later still, to Macedonia. We remained here about four years, and then removed to Nauvoo, where we assisted in the building of the Temple, was intimate with the Prophet, and often received instruction from his own lips. While residing here, my brother Amos d ed; my sisters Mary and Esther, and my brother Joseph, and I were married. In 1843 the mob burned houses, destroyed property, and drove the Saints from place to place. Joseph and Hyrum Smith were imprisoned in the Jail at Carthage and on June 29th 1844 pas murdered by a mob, while under a pledge of the State for protection. About this time the Laws, Fosters, Higbees and others, with John C. Bennett (a consummate villian) at their head, turned against the Church and the Prophet. When the Saints were banished from the State, I, with a few others, remained to care for abandoned property. Witnessed the burning of the Temple. In Spring of 1850 I started westward to gather with the family and friends at Kanesville, Iowa, whither several of them had already gone. Here I remained until the Spring of 1851, engaged in visiting and caring for the sick, this being the great year of the Cholera, when thousands fell victim to its ravages.

In the Spring of 1851 I started, with my wife and children, for the Rocky Mountains (Utah,) where my brothers Joel and Benjamin had already gone, and after a long and tedious journey we arrived in the Valley of the Great Salt Lake in October, 1851. After remaining in the city a few days I moved on to Summit Creek, (afterwards Santaquin,) in Utah County, where my brother Benjamin had been called to establish a colony. There I built the first cabin

In January, 1852, the Indians becoming hostile, we abandoned Santaquin and moved to Springville, that we might better defend ourselves. When peace was again restored, I was called to assist in the building up of Iron County. Here, in connection with my nephew, Nephi Johnson, we compiled, for publication, the Pah-Ute dialect, and in the Winter of 1855 I went to Salt Lake City and had it printed. On my return, I was snow-bound in the mountains, and suffered very much, being almost entirely without food for four days.

I remained in Iron Co., about two years, and then returned to Santaquin (which had been demolished by the Indians,) to assist in re-building the town. This being the great Grasshopper year, I did not raise any grain, and was obliged to spend the Winter in Iron Co.; returned to Santaquin in Spring of 1857, having with me enough flour to last my family, and others through the famine of this year. While here, I was appointed councilor to Bishop Jas. S. Holman; also, clerk of the Branch, which position I filled until the Summer of 1859, when I was called to pioneer a settlement in the Uintah Springs, in Sanpete County. During the Summer I laid off the town of Fountaingreen, and prepared for building. In the Fall the colony began to arrive, and I was appointed Bishop. I remained here till the Summer of 1861, when I returned to Santaquin, and there remained until 1864, when I removed to Spring Lake Villa, where my brother Joseph had settled. In the Spring of 1865 I went to the Eastern States on business—to purchase goods &c.; came near losing life, teams and supplies, but was preserved, with loss of a few articles which floated out of wagon. Reached Council Bluffs, Iowa, after being 30 days away from home. Spent a month fitting up teams, and buying goods, and started on the return trip about the middle of July. When a few days out on our journey, we began to hear of an Indian outbreak, and meet the Rancheros coming in to the settlements for protection. At Fort Kearney we were detained by the troops, with all the emigration, for nearly six weeks. The remainder of the journey was through scenes of desolation; the ranchos devastated, people murdered,—everything abandoned to the Indians and wolves. Arrived in Salt Lake City in November, having left part of our stock and goods at various places along the road, and suffered everything but death.

The next Summer, I was called to go South, to assist in opening up new sections of the country, and making new settlements. I sold out and fitted up for the trip, but was prevented from going by sickness, and loss of stock.

In the Spring of 1867, I removed to Mona, Juab Co., where I have lived up to the time of this writing, June 1st, 1882.

At the close of this sketch, I will briefly say, that I became acquainted with the Prophet Joseph Smith in the Spring of 1833, and was intimate with him until his death, and can truly say that I ever found him loyal to his country, true to his friends, upright in his dealings and intercourse with all men; a good neighbor and an agreeable companion.

GEORGE W. JOHNSON.

MONA, UTAH, JUNE 1st 1882.

LINES, WRITTEN

· BY ·

JAMES H. MARTINEAU.

TRUTH.

A blooming flower, in beauty bright,
A dew-drop, glistening in the light,
May fade, or vanish from the sight,
    Nor leave a trace behind:
But Truth—eternal, priceless Truth—
The brightest gem that's found on earth,
Though ages roll, yet still in youth,
    Will shine with light Divine.

It gives a knowledge of the past,
The present, and the future vast;
It lives, and will forever last,
    Though *Time* may pass away.
Then, if we're wise, this gem we'll seek,
And when 'tis found, securely keep,
Nor shut our eyes in slumber deep—
    Nor shun its heavenly ray.

TWILIGHT MEMORIES.

'Tis eve: the sunlight gilds with golden hue
The snowy, cloud-encircled mountain top,
And in the darkening shadowy dale, the dew
    On flower and leaflet gathers, drop by drop.
Now, all is silent, save the murmuring rill
That leaps along its steep and rocky bed,
Or save the distant, faintly tinkling bell—
    Or soft-winged bat that circles round my head.

The visions of the past before me rise,
And oft are happy,—oft so sadly sweet,
That tears unbidden, glisten in my eyes,
  At thought of those whom I no more shall meet.
I see again my Father's reverend form—
His grave demeanor, and his stately air,
His sparkling eye, with love and friendship warm—
  The forehead—crowned with silver-sprinkled hair.

My Mother! ah, how sacred is that word!
The first that by the infant lip is spoken,
The last that on the battle field is heard
  From thousands, ere their thread of life is broken.
I see again her kind and loving face
That o'er me bent in childhoods blissful slumbers—
Her gently beaming eye, her quiet grace;—
  Ah, who can e'er those happy mem'ries number!

I hear again a spirit-whispered song
A sister used to sing, while at her feet
We nestled closely round. Her voice hath long
  Been silent now;—the cold, white, winding-sheet
Enwraps our loved one's form, and on the stone
Her name engraven is with moss o'ergrown.
A lily pure and spotless, blooming bright;   [sight.
Life's spring awhile she graced—then passed from

I had a brother once—a baby boy
Scarce two years old, with soft and gentle eye,
And wavy hair—his mother's latest joy;
  And happy as the bird that caroled nigh.
Years since have passed: I never saw him more,
But have been told that on the battle plain
When rushing armies trampled deep in gore
He fell among our country's valiant slain!
  No purer patriotism than his was found,—
  No braver heart our banner gathered round.

How many tried and trusted friends are gone!
How many times our aching hearts have bled!
How oft an old and half-remembered song
  Hath brought to mind these scenes forever fled.

A FEW NOTES FROM THE LIFE OF

J. E. JOHNSON.

Was born in Pomfret, Chatauqua Co., New York, on the 28th day of April, 1817. Moved to Kirtland in 1832. Baptized as a Latter-Day Saint in 1833. Went with the Kirtland Camp in 1838. Taught school in Springfield, Ill. in 1839. Went to Nauvoo in 1840. Married to Harriet Snyder, by Joseph Smith in 1841. Accompanied Joseph and Hyrum Smith on their way to Carthage Jail. Was taken prisoner when mob entered Nauvoo. Went to "Miller's Hollow" (now Council Bluffs) in 1848. Built the first house in Pottawatamie County. Was postmaster at Council Bluffs for five years, and obtained a change of name from "Kanesville" to Council Bluffs. Was a member of first City Council for several years. Established the *Council Bluffs Bugle* in 1852. Office and store destroyed by fire in 1853. Restored and published until 1856. The *Bugle* had much to do in getting the Capitol of Nebraska located at Omaha. Was elected to the Nebraska Legislature, but was too much of a Democrat to get a seat. Opened the first store on the site of Omaha, and sent the first train of goods to the Denver Colorado, (Cherry Creek) mines. In '54 published the *Omaha Arrow*, the first paper published on Nebraska soil, and the same year accompanied the first party of explorers for a railroad crossing on the Missouri River and Loupe Fork of Platte River. Wrote the first article published favoring the North Platte route for the Pacific Rail Road, and contended for same until so located, (*vide* files of *Bugle*.) Crossed the Plains to Utah and back in 1850. In 1857 started the *Crescent City Oracle* and laid out the town of that name. In 1858 published the *Council Bluffs Press*. In 1859—'60—'61 published the *Huntsman's Echo* at

Wood River, Neb. In 1861 removed to Utah. In '63 published the *Farmer's Oracle* at Spring Lake Villa, Utah County. In 1865 removed to Saint George, and began a supply garden and and nursery. In 1868—'69 published *Our Dixie Times,* afterwards the *Rio Virgen Times.* In 1870 published the *Utah Pomologist and Gardener,* monthly, for several years. In 1876 went to Silver Reef and put up store and printing office, but sold part of office before paper was fairly started. In 1879 was burned out, with many others. Restored store immediately, on larger scale. In 1880 began to look southward for new homes, and to-morrow, June 24th, 1882, with the blessings of Providence, I shall start in company with my brother B. F., for the land of Old Mexico, to open up, ere I pass from this life, a place of refuge for the Saints of God.

Have three wives, and am the father of 26 children, 16 of whom are now living, and have 27 grandchildren, 19 now living.   J. E. JOHNSON.
ST. GEORGE, UTAH, JUNE 23RD, 1882.

LINES, WRITTEN ON VARIOUS OCCASIONS

BY

JOSEPH E. JOHNSON.

OUR BOYHOOD'S HOME.

'Tis Christmas, Brothers dear, to-day,
    And like, in scenes of early years,
The earth is mantled white with snow,
    And brooklets gleam with icy tears;
        And bells ring out in merry chime,
        As erst in our young Christmas time.

My thoughts are wandering far away
    To days of boyhood's brightest dreams,

When on each "Merry Christmas" day,
  We coasted on the hills and streams:
    And merry shout, and laugh did there
    Ring out upon the wint'ry air.

At eve our Christmas dinner smoked
  Upon the cross-legg'd table old;--
Goose, turkey, spare-rib, chicken pie,
  And Indian pudding gleaming gold;
    With pies of mince and pumpkin too,
    We ate, as boys alone could do.

And then, for playmates gathered oft,
  For evening games and kissing plays;
How sweetly passed those joyous scenes,
  Those long gone, happy Christmas days:
    Embalmed in Memory's sacred shrine.
    The joys of boyhood's happy time.

Our Christmas fires! how bright they glowed,
  Within the fire-place broad and high,
Where crane and hooks swung dinner pot
  And kettle for the nut-cake fry:
    And porringer and trencher clean,
    In every rural home were seen.

In spring we boiled the maple's sap,
  And gathered wild flowers blooming fair,
And merry boys and girls would meet,
  To "sugar off" in wildwood there;
    And when the spring-time glories fade,
    We hunted berries in the glade.

In meadows verdant, waving, green,
  We searched for strawberries, sweet and red,
The Gulf-farm grew sweet wintergreens,
  Whose berries there were thickly spread;
    For birch bark, gum, and slippery elm,
    We traversed oft our boyhood's realm.

And when the cherries, smiling red,
  Were gleaming in the summer breeze,

How we enjoyed the dainty feast,
　The while, we pluck them from the trees;
　　Of gooseberries, and currants rare,
　　We seldom failed to get our share.

In summer's heat, the hay we stirred,
　To pasture drove the lowing cows,
And from the orchard gathered fruit,
　And ate it 'neath the shady boughs;
　　In autumn, through the leafy grove,
　　For mandrakes, plums, and grapes we'd rove.

In Casadaga's lake we fished
　And gathered lilies—fragrant flowers;
And on blue Erie's beaten shore,
　Spent many bright and happy hours;
　　Anh later, to Fredonia's Square,
　　We ne'er missed "General Training" there.

When frost had nipp'd the leafy trees
　That Chestnuts from the burs might fall,
And nuts from Beech and But'nut trees,
　Black Walnuts, Hickory-nuts and all,
　　When winds were high we took a run
　　For nuts, for winter eves to come.

The dear old School house near the wood,
　The teachers, scholars, books and plays,
All vanished! from the dear old spot,
　Gone! disappeared in various ways,
　　And scarce a vestige now is seen,
　　Of what our boy-time home had been.

The Mother dear! that watched our youth,
　The Father kind, the Sisters loved,
The Brothers brave, the playmates fond,
　With whom, in youth's bright time we moved,
　　Gone! to a sunnier, happier home,
　　Or in far distant lands they roam.

STAR OF HOPE.

As shades of eve are softly stealing,
  O'er the flowery landscape bright;
Glittering diamond orbs revealing,
  Smiling goddess, Queen of Night.

Yonder gloomy, dark clouds hovering,
  Shedding forth their drenching showers,
Sombre frowns, gay nature covering,—
  Bringing life to slumbering flowers.

Thus the wint'ry frosts so chilling,
  Bring to flowers and field-plants green,
Quiet sleep, from which, more smiling,
  Come they forth in loveliest sheen.

So, from darkest clouds of sorrow,
  Gleams anon Hope's brilliant star,
Promise of a bright to-morrow,
  Doubling joys for every care.

From the mines most deep and fearful,
  Diamonds rich, and ores are found,
From the eyes most sad and tearful,
  Loving treasures oft abound.

FAIR VALE OF DESERET. 1851.

Thou beauteous vale! awhile farewell!
  Where late with kindred Saints I've met;
Where all in love and union dwell—
  Thou charming Land of Deseret.

A land like this, is no where found
  From rising sun to where it set,
No! not so sweet the earth around,
  As this sweet vale of Deseret.

Thy mountain peaks so wild and high,
  With cooling showers are often wet;

Their snow-capp'd summits reach the sky,
  None wild and fair as Deseret.

Thy crystal streams are cool and pure,
  Their rippling course makes music sweet;
With earth their fountains will endure—
  Ye sparkling brooks of Deseret.

The Saints, within thy wall of rocks,
  Their distant friends will ne'er forget;
But haste the growth of grain and flocks,
  To help them forth to Deseret.

All dwell in peace in this dear vale,
  With foes and fears no more beset;
No cries of want, nor poor to wail
  Within thy borders, Deseret,

Soon to thy peaceful shades once more
  I'll come—I leave thee with regret—
And seek a humble, quiet home,
  Vale of the Saints, sweet Deseret.

———————

LINES WRITTEN DURING A STORM ON THE MISSOURI RIVER IN 1851.

Without, the rain in fitful torrents pour,
  And hoarse the wrathful wind doth moan aloud;
The lightnings flash, the crashing thunders roar,
  Majestic in their might amid the clouds.

All nature seems to mark the passing night
  With darksome shades and gloomy reveries;
And not a planet cheers us with its light,
  Nor marks the place of heaven's bright liveries.

Our barque is tossed upon the waters dark,
  Where snags and wrecks in wild confusion lay,
With not a beacon, it's lone path to mark;
  No light but heaven's electric, piercing ray.

My spirit pines for one congenial soul,
  One ray of friendship's bright ethereal gleam;
Waters and storms, and thunders then might roll,
  We'd glide, still happy, down this turbid stream.

THE GRAVES OF MY KINDRED.
Written while visiting our Old Home in Kirtland, Ohio, December, 1851.

I stood by the graves of my kindred, so dear,
  Where the greensward had closely o'erspread,
My eyes were bedimmed with memory's sad tear,
  As I gazed on the tombs of the dead.

Two brothers were sleeping in death's cold domain,
  How dear doth their memory cling;
Though lost to sad friends, free from sorrow and pain,
  In the haven where death cannot sting.

How kindly they watched o'er my once tender years,
  Such kindness one ne'er can forget;
How oft in my dreams I embrace them, with tears,
  Their images dwell with me yet.

Two, dear, lovely sisters, were laid in the ground,
  By the side of the brothers they loved;
In sacred affection their lives here were bound,
  Nor severed in bright realms above.

Those kind, gentle sisters! how patient and meek,
  When affliction and pain was severe;
How often in sweet, gentle tones they would speak,
  Our childhoods *deep heart-griefs* to cheer.

Long, long years estranged from the land where they
      sleep,
  Once again on the sad spot I've gazed;
In sorrow I ponder,—o'er their graves let me weep,

To the mem'ry of life's happier days.
O'er the hill where they lie we have oft roamed for
    pleasure,
On the fruit of the orchard have often regaled,
The sweet, blooming, gardens perfume was a treasure,
As daily, it's fragrance at eve, we inhaled.

The garden, the orchard, and the place where they rest,
    And the once happy circle's loved home
In Kirtland, is now by rude strangers possessed,
    Alas! how much changed 'tis become.

From a bough that grew o'er them, memento I have,
    A relic both sacred and dear;
Oh may we prove guiltless when called from the grave,
    And with them, and the righteous, appear.

REMEMBER, LOVE, REMEMBER.

Remember, love, remember—
That life is but a transient stream,
Of Springtime's bloom and Autumn's gleam,
A barque upon life's varied stream,
    'Tis Maytime and December.
Be thine the radiant Spring and flowers,
Where sweet birds chant in fragrant bowers.

Remember, love, remember—
That time is but a fleeting day,
For life and love a flowering May,
Where hope for sweetest blossoms stray,
    Quick comes the sere September;
And Winter hastes, with silent tread,
And we are numbered with the dead.

Remember, love, remember,—
That beauty's breath is on the wing,
That vanity will leave its sting,
That folly no true pleasures bring,

But sorrow will attend her;
That pride and fame will leave no trace
To mark their gilded restingplace.
    Remember, love, O! mind it,—
That if we strew with thorns our bed,
A rocky pillow for our head,
We cannot hope for down instead,
    Nor shall we ever find it;
But every piercing thorn we sow
Shall form a garland for our brow.

    Remember, love, remember,
That if we cause a pang of woe
To kindred mortals here below,
Doubly the sorrow we shall know,
    When our accounts we render;
That if we would be loved, must learn
To live in truth, and love in turn.

    Remember, love, our reason
Is given for a purpose great,
Our lives on earth to elevate,
That we may know that happier state,
    When we have spent life's season;
And every generous deed of love
Shall glitter in our crown above.

    Remember, love, remember,
Affections, richer far than gold,
May faint with slight or chill with cold,
That purest passions ever told,
    May fade in bleak November;
That fuel keeps a' glowing flame,
Affection must be fed the same.

THE DREAMER.

My eyes the God of Sleep did close,
    And all was hushed in deep repose;

My dreamy thoughts quick made their flight
  Beyond the shades of gloom of night.

I saw my dearly cherished home,
  From which, far distant, now I roam;
My kind, though aged mother, dear,
  My wives and children all, were near.

My sisters loved, and brothers kind,
  All came distinctly to my mind;
I kissed them each, and warmly pressed
  Their hands—and clasped them to my breast.

So happy in their joyous smile,
  All seemed *so* real—*so* free from guile.
I told of places where I'd been,
  And talked and laughed at what was seen.

But list! what music breaks the spell?
  It is the Porter's breakfast bell
That breaks the pleasant, magic chain,
  And sends me far from home again.

THE OLD SCHOOL HOUSE.

The following lines were suggested on receipt, by the
author, of a relic of "the old School House on
the hill" a few days since.

DEDICATED TO HIS OLD SCHOOL-MATES.

How sweet the lingering dreams of olden time
Of childhood's spring in far-off native clime,
'Mid wild Chatauqua's hills we used to stray,
Where wood-nymph fairies held a magic sway.

Our cot was high away from Erie's shore,
Too far to hear the storm tossed waters' roar;
Yet white sails dotting o'er the lake's clear blue,
Were often ready to our wondering view.

How oft in dreams we lightly trip, at dawn,
Where sparkling dews illume the grassy lawn.
For dandelions, cowslips, daisies gay,
Or to cull berries midst the growing hay.

How oft, we've marked the hills with boyish feet,
For fragrant wintergreens, with berries sweet;
And by the fields for blackberries we've roved,
With red-cheeked schoolmates that we fondly loved,

The village bell, though full three miles away,
We heard distinctly on each new-born day;
It's peal, more solemn on the Sabbath air,
Marked time for school, for service and for prayer.

The school-house! ah! the red one on the hill,
Full two miles South, Laona's noisy mill;
Midway between the two we met our birth,
Our boyhood thought the brightest spot on earth.

How oft we've met, with laughing girls and boys;
The happiest those who made the greatest noise;
Till Master came, with rule in hand, to bring.
Order again, as beaten clapboards ring.

To books and study then with earnest will—
We learned to spell, to read, and wield the quill;
And once a week, through wint'ry frost or sleet,
At spelling-school each playmate we did greet.

In Autumn, when the mellow fruit was red,
To "paring-bees" with lightened step we tread;
Where hopeful lads in home-spun hues were dressed,
In gaudy prints the lasses looked their best.

We peeled the fruit, told yarns, and joked and laughed,
We kissed the girls—new cider then we quaffed,
Then mince and pumpkin-pies, and cakes were spread,
And then we played and laughed till night had sped.

Then homeward we with blushing fair ones go,

And little else but happiness did know.
Alas! those school-mates now are scattered wide!
Some have grown great, and others pined and died!

Away, 'mid Rocky Mountains' peaks and snows!
Thanks! schoolmate, thanks! for relic of the house
Where oft we've met our joyous playmate band.
Memento cherished, of my native land.

THE PRAIRIE FIRE.

Listen! hist! what sound so dread,
Thundering like the earthquake's tread?
Wide the rumbling echoes spread,
          The Prairie Fire!

See the darksome cloud ascend,
Like the breath of some foul fiend,
As o'er earth in wrath it bends;
          The Prairie Fire!

Hark! the hissing roar comes near,—
Fills the stoutest heart with fear;
Swiftly fly the frightened Deer,
          The Prairie Fire!

Hear the crackling, fearful sound
As the rapid flames rebound,—
Lighting up the darkness round;
          The Prairie Fire!

Now subsiding, now it rears,—
As the tall, dry grass it nears,
Flashes high—then disappears;
          The Prairie Fire!

Now, 'tis moving calm and slow;
O'er the hills the bright flames go
Like a serpent;—all aglow,
          The Prairie Fire!

Now, the sky with radiance bright
Back reflects the lurid light,
Making day of darkest night,
        The Prairie Fire!

THE TELEGRAPH.

A Recitation given at a Party in St. George, Utah,
celebrating the completion of the line of the
"Deseret Telegraph Co." to that place,
in the Winter (January) of 1867.

From Mississippi's verdant slopes, some twenty years
    ago,
The Saints from pleasant homes were driven, amid
    the wint'ry snows;
They took their course o'er deserts wild, across the
    trackless plains,
With *graves* they sadly marked their way, through
    storms and chilling rains.

They reached the briny inland sea, amid the mountain
    vales,
Where quiet reigned, except the wolves' and Indian's
    yells and wails;
The land was desert, parched and sere, and salt the
    virgin soil,
With faith in God, these weary few went forth to earn-
    est toil.

What are they now?—an hundred leagues, with fields
    and orchards green,
An hundred cities rise to view, an hundred spires are
    seen;
And grain and fruits, and vines and plants, and flow-
    ers of gorgeous hue,
And flocks and herds, o'er vales and hills are seen at
    every view.

To-night a chain of thought is laid, from northern,
    snowy lands,
To "Dixie's" cheerful, sunny clime, to Virgen's glitter-
    ing sands;
A ray of Light through Deseret, electric, Heavenly
    glow,
Through which the words of faith and hope, and end-
    less life, may flow.
God bless the Chief, the men and boys, and we must
    not forget
The sisters who assisted too—the pride of Deseret!
And may the Saints e'er grateful prove, for every bless-
    ing given,
And for this thread of light and thought, between the
    Earth and Heaven.

"SHOW US A SIGN AND WE WILL BELIEVE."

INCIDENTS IN EARLY LIFE.

BY BENJAMIN F. JOHNSON.

About the year 1830, when I was twelve years of age, Nancy, my eldest sister was thrown from a horse and her hip broken, the bone breaking so near the socket it could not be set, and physicians all agreed that it would be impossible for her ever again to walk upon that leg, or in any degree to recover its use, as ossification had taken place without a connection of the bones, and they had slipped past each other, making the broken limb nearly an inch shorter than the other. She walked on two crutches, and for years was not able to bring upon the broken limb weight to hurt the finger of a small child if placed under her foot. In the year 1831 my brothers Joel and David received the gospel in Amherst, Ohio, and in the Fall of the same year my brother Joel brought to us the Book of Mormon, at Fredonia, N. Y. Soon after, A. W. Babbit, then but a boy, came also, followed by Elders Brackenbury and Durfee. Elder Brackenbury was an earnest and powerful preacher, and seemed filled with the spirit of the Lord, many receiving the testimony of the three elders. My Mother, with Lyman R. Sherman (a brother-in-law) were the first to be baptized. Priests and people began to oppose the work, and would scoffingly ask "why, if miracles can be performed, do you not heal sister Nancy?" and many would say, "oh, yes, if they would only heal her, we all would believe." My sister was a young woman of excellent mind and character. Having a good common-school education, she had for some years taught our district school, and being religiously inclined, had joined the Free-will Baptist Church, and, like my Mother, who was also a religious woman, was not only respected, but beloved by all who knew her. Altho' she had obeyed the gospel, the time had not come for her deliverance from crutches by the healing power of God. The wicked were seeking it for a sign as in the days of our Saviour, when they followed him even to his crucifixion, demanding that he come down from the cross as a sign to prove to them that he was the Son of God, yet no sign was given except that of their overthrow and destruction.

After a few weeks of successful preaching and baptising, Elder Brackenbury was taken violently sick, and within a few days died of billious colic. To us, young and inexperienced members in the Church, his death came as a trial to our faith, as well as a great grief. To think so good a man, in so useful a field of labor, far away from his home and family, should be permitted to die, and so suddenly, was designed as a test to the faith and integrity of so young a branch. Although the grave had closed over his body, and we were in deep sorrow, our enemies were not satisfied, for while we were assembled in the evening after his burial, to talk and pray, and mourn together, the fact was revealed to my brother David that the body was being molested. Hastening, with others, to the place of burial, about one mile distant, they discovered several men (two or three), just preparing to hoist the coffin from the grave. On hearing their approach the ghouls fled, but were pursued, and one (a young medical student) was captured. He was committed by a magistrate, but nothing further done about it.

Soon after this we concluded to leave our native place and gather with the Saints at Kirtland, Ohio, which we did in the Spring of 1833, in the Summer of which year it was decided to build a Temple, of brick, and my three eldest brothers, assisted by we who were younger, began the task of making the bricks for the purpose, and here David, then about 22 years of age, became a martyr to the great and good cause, through his ambition to perform more labor than his body was capable of enduring, and by over-exertion in procuring the wood, he bled at the lungs, and died the same Fall, bearing a faithful testimony to the truth of the gospel, and speaking in the Gift of Tongues with his latest breath, which was readily interpreted by Don Carlos Smith, a brother of the Prophet, who was, at the time, present.

About this time the Spirit of the Lord seemed to be poured out upon the Saints in Kirtland;—families often assembled to "speak of the Lord," and the gifts of the Gospel were enjoyed in rich abundance. As yet my sister Nancy had never taken a step since her fall, unaided by crutches, but the time of her deliverance had now come, and she was commanded by Elder Jared Carter, then a man of mighty faith, to arise, leave her crutches, and walk. She arose in faith, full of joy, and was from that hour made whole, and never again did she walk upon a crutch or lean upon a staff.

www.ingramcontent.com/pod-product-compliance
Lightning Source LLC
Chambersburg PA
CBHW031244260626
47169CB00007B/2437